The Nest of Chockablock Hair

The friendship of a girl who can't hear and a bird who can't speak

Illustrated by
Monica Paterson
& Eve Farb

by Linda Teed

This book is dedicated to the amazing albatross – this most unique, perfect bird – and its Creator, who thinks of absolutely everything; who inspires me and sends the most amazing people my way.

You, Lord, are my anchor.
PRT...we'll keep walking

goose water press

Published by Goose Water Press LLC.
www.kristenemilybehl.com

ISBN:
e-Book: 978-1-954809-19-2
Paperback: 978-1-954809-18-5
Hardcover: 978-1-954809-17-8

Original character illustrations of Maria and Louie copyright Eve Farb via Creative Market. All additional characters and background illustrations by Monica Paterson.

Why is this book written in Six Word Form?

Six Word Form is born from a style of poetry called Six Word Memoir. A Six Word Memoir poem consists of six words written as a phrase or sentence that expresses a deep thought or emotion. My use of the Six Word Form style of writing began in my classroom. Just as there are reluctant readers, there are reluctant writers. I wanted to give my students an opportunity to write with fewer words and rules. The Six Word Form provides freedom for a young writer to express themselves with less fear of failure.

She plays **alone** on the shore.

ADVENTURE calls her, sea spray thrills!

RUGGED WINDS gust, sand blows hither-tither

Delightful quiet wonder; her silent playground.

A noiseless **W🌎RLD;**
LONELINESS
surrounds her.

Kids with words
don't play here.

Her spirit
yearns to be

SHARED.

SUDDENLY
from above, a fluttery
thwump!

She glances up,
he glances down.

Moves right in,
flumps right down
in a nest of
chockablock hair.

He twitches,
wings flap clumsily
OFF-KILTER;

a short fall to her lap.

His eyes **GRATEFUL,** her eyes stunned.

He hears her,
somehow,
without
words.

She giggles and **HUGS** him close,

their smiles **wide** as the ocean.

They dance and cause a ruckus.

Pure joy, for she is understood!

A silent girl
BURSTING with love,

her mighty  HEART
thrumming a path.

For the lost can be found;

HOPE will lead
the way home.

Maria, Louie... LEARNING, SEARCHING, FORGING, DISCOVERING.

UNLOCKING the secrets of buried treasure

Learning about the albatross's GIANT wings;

Schools of fish,
delicious
meal.

EXPERIENCING the stars'
bright twinkling light-

a **LIGHT** that destroys the **DARKNESS.**

Reading about princesses SCARY and dragons

damsels in DISTRESS and BRAVE KNIGHTS

Singing about wishes and HEARTS desires.

They
PLAY
and
SCREECH
and
GUFFAW.

They breathe and WISH and pretend.

They learn and GROW
STRONGER together,

and together both
learn to FLY.

Time slips through the sand's hourglass.

Waves once **HARSH** become sweet, mellow.

The road once BUMPY made SMOOTH-

YET the lost **YEARN** to be found.

EXHAUSTED parents search day and night.

Their DETERMINATION never wavers or warps.

One sunny day, thunderous commotion ERUPTS!

Deafening **GIGGLES** turn searching heads downward.

Warbling BREAKS through the clouds above,

and birds, together, hear familiar **SQUAWKS**

and the loud thrumming of **HEARTS.**

Then, an
EXPLOSION
of birdy trills!

Wings spread **wide** as the sky,

an albatross CELEBRATION like no other.

UNBRIDLED **JOY;** his family together **again!**

Through sadness,
through hope,
RESOLVE.

DELIGHT,

Maria no longer **LONELY**,
but CONFIDENT.

Louie no longer LOST, but FOUND.

An inner strength,
a gentle FIRE.

for **tRue LOVe** knows no distance.

Her bird, his girl,

forever connected.

And silent doors now open **wide:**

NEW FRIENDSHIPS to create and **explore,**

FOREVER TOGETHER, the sweet baby albatross

and the girl with chockablock hair.

Linda Teed lives in a humble little township in the beautiful USA, where she and her husband Patrick raised up three extraordinary kids and earned the new title of grandparents.

When she's not teaching and creating, you'll find her at the library surrounded by all her friends. She dares to "sing about wishes and hearts' desires" and marvels at "the stars' bright twinkling light – a light that destroys the darkness."

Monica is native to South Africa. Together with her husband, she has raised three young men who – apart from the crazy math guy – share her talent for creativity.

Having lived on 3 continents in the last 16 years, as an artist she draws inspiration from the many different places and cultures she has experienced. Monica now focuses on teaching art and pursuing her passion in illustrating children's books and freelance Graphic Design.

Free supplemental resources! Just follow this link!

https://monster365.myportfolio.com

Lightning Source UK Ltd.
Milton Keynes UK
UKHW050901071221
395218UK00002B/24